Hi, I'm Dar

It's Tuesday and we've got swimming.

That's Mr Woods with our group.

He's our teacher.

He wants me to try to swim a length

today. I said I would have a go.

I must be mad!

I've got changed, and now I'm in
the pool.
I'm practising in the shallow end.

I don't like swimming much.
It's all right in the shallow end.
I can do a width, no problem.
Last week I did three widths without
stopping.
I didn't touch the bottom once!

What I don't like about swimming is...

Getting changed in front of everyone and having showers.

People splashing or bumping into me.

I don't like it when the water is freezing.

I *hate* it when I can't touch the bottom.

That's really scary!

I'm in the deep end now, and this is it!
The water is really deep and I'm feeling
nervous.
Is it too late to say no?
I could say I'm not well.
I look at Mr Woods.
No, that's not a good idea!

1,2,3…I'm off!

I've done the first few strokes.

I'm feeling OK.

I hope I can keep going like this.

There's still miles to go.

Oh no! Something has gone wrong.

Water has gone up my nose and

I've swallowed a bucketful.

My legs start to sink.

Relax? You must be joking!

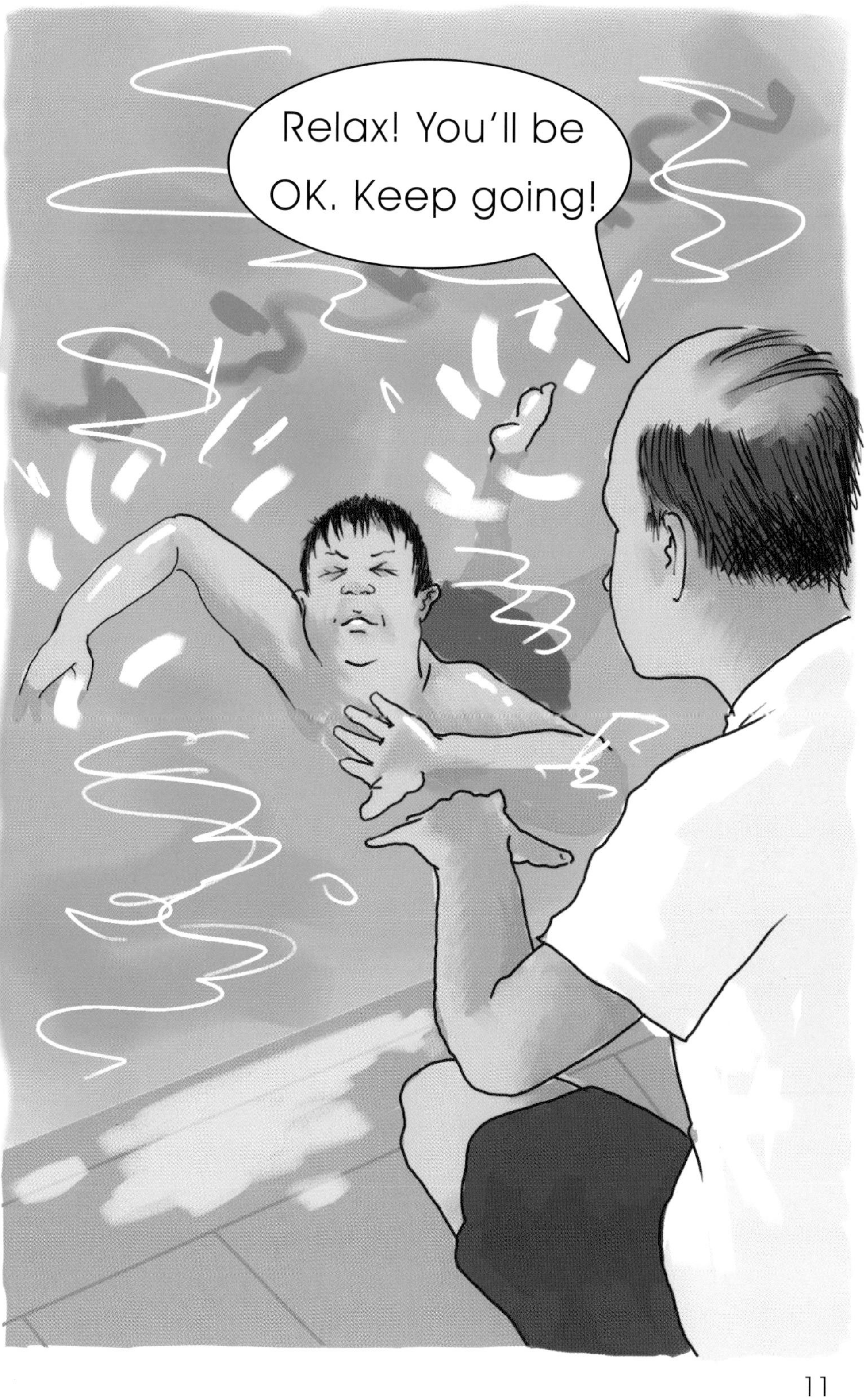
Relax! You'll be OK. Keep going!

Everything is OK again, and I'm halfway.

My arms and legs are starting to ache.

I can hear someone coming up
behind me.

Is it Susie? What's she doing? She's going
to crash into me.

I can hear Mr Woods shouting to her and
she moves away.

It's not far to go now.

I'm knackered! Sorry! Very tired.

I can hear lots of shouting and cheering.

I'm nearly there…just a few more strokes.

Well done, Darren!

You were great!

I've made it!

I've swum a whole length!

Everyone is saying "Well done!"

I feel FANTASTIC!

Just wait till I tell my dad!

Do you think Darren will start to like swimming now?